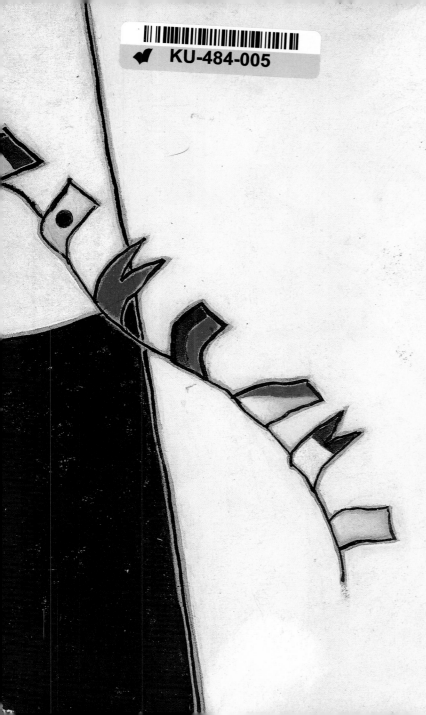

For Rik

First published in the Netherlands in 2000 by Querido's Uitgeverij B.V.
First published in Great Britain in 2003 by Macmillan Children's Books
a division of Pan Macmillan Publishers Limited
20 New Wharf Road, London N1 9RR
Basingstoke and Oxford
Associated companies worldwide
www.panmacmillan.com

ISBN 0 333 98735 7 (HB)
ISBN 0 333 99290 3 (PB)

A CIP catalogue record for this book is available
from the British Library.

Printed in Belgium

BURY METRO LIBRARIES

This book must be returned on or before the last date
recorded below to the Library from which it was borrowed.

17. JUN. 2003		MAR - 6 2009
20. NOV. 2003	17. AUG. 2003	2 3 NOV 2009
27 NOV. 2003	1 8 NOV 2006	- 8 FEB 2010
15. JUN 2004	- 2 MAR 2007	2 7 JAN 2011
-4. OCT. 2004		
-4. APR.	- 7 JAN 2008	2 8 FEB 2011
23. SEP 2005	JUL 1 2 2008	3 0 APR 2013
-1. NOV. 2005	NOV - 4 2008	1 8 NOV 2013
		2 0 FEB 2014
		2 2 FEB 2024

AUTHOR

TITLE

CLASS No.

Hello, Sailor

Ingrid Godon

with words by André Sollie

MACMILLAN CHILDREN'S BOOKS

Matt's lighthouse was so big that he could live inside it.

Each night, he lit the great lamp to guide the ships safely home.

People felt safe when they saw the bright light shining in the dark.

People far out to sea, like Sailor.

Rose lived on the edge of the sand dunes. Every morning she brought Matt bread and cheese for his lunch. Sometimes she brought a slice of cake as well, or a kipper.

Matt was too busy to go shopping. He had to keep a lookout over the sea. But mostly Matt kept a lookout for Sailor.

One day Sailor had gone to sea.

"I'll come back for you," Sailor had said when he left. "Then we'll sail round the world together, just you and me."

"Matt!" Rose shouted into the wind. "I've brought your bread!" There was no reply. Rose sighed. "Forget about Sailor," she said. "I'm sure he's forgotten about you. I bet he's lying on a beach somewhere, or lying at the bottom of the sea!"

The wind blew fiercely. It almost knocked Felix over as he walked up the
dunes to deliver Matt's post. Matt used to chat to Felix, but he didn't have
time any more. He was too busy staring at the ships that passed.

Matt would never forget what Sailor's ship looked like. And he'd never forget what Sailor looked like, either.

"Matt!" shouted Felix. "I've got a letter for you!"

"Is it from Sailor?"

"No, it's from Emma. Oh, you and your Sailor! I bet he's been swallowed by a whale. Or captured by pirates!"

"Can you open the letter for me, Felix?" Matt shouted from the top of the lighthouse.

"Awww!" squawked Seagull. "Awww!"

"It is from Emma," Felix yelled over the noise. "She's coming to visit. It's your birthday tomorrow!"

"So it is!" said Matt. "Let's have a party. You're both invited. See you tomorrow, Felix. See you tomorrow, Rose."

Matt had forgotten all about his birthday.
He had been too busy thinking about
Sailor. "I bet he'll come back tomorrow,"
Matt thought. "In time for my birthday.
And then they'll see."

"Awww!" said Seagull.

Matt found some bunting in a chest
to decorate the lighthouse. "We'll need a
cake, too," he said to himself. "And some
rum. Sailor loves rum."

The next day, the wind had dropped and the sun was shining brightly.

Felix gave Matt a ship in a bottle and Rose brought a big box of chocolates.
Emma's present was a real sailor's jumper that she had knitted herself.

"It's for when Sailor comes back," she explained. "For when you sail off together."

"That's right." Matt smiled. "We're going to sail round the world together."

Felix played a jolly tune on the accordion and everyone began to sing and dance.

But nobody opened the bottle of rum and Matt's new jumper felt scratchy.

Matt went to check that the lighthouse lamp was properly lit. "After all," he thought, "Sailor won't be able to find his way in the dark."

Later that night, when the stars were shining and the guests had gone home to bed, a man walked over the sand to the lighthouse.

"Matt!" he called, in a loud whisper.
"Are you awake?" There was no answer.
"Ahoy there!"

But the wind was so strong, it carried
his words away.

The man went inside the lighthouse and climbed the steep spiral staircase. His heart was pounding.

"Matt?" he called again. Still no reply. He opened the door quietly.

"Sailor!" Matt gasped. "You've come back!" He couldn't believe his eyes. "Hello, Sailor!"

Sailor laughed. "Did you think I'd forgotten you? I thought we were going to sail round the world together."

"Yes," cried Matt. "I've been waiting for you!"

The two friends didn't know whether to laugh or cry. They turned round in a circle, to get a better look at one another. It was almost as if they were dancing.

Sailor was back!

They sat outside beneath the stars and ate leftover cake and drank some rum.
Sailor told Matt stories about the sea and the faraway countries he had visited,
and about how they were going to sail round the world together.

It was almost dawn when Matt and Sailor finally made their way down to the boat.

"Awww!" screeched Seagull. He was going, too. "Awww!"

It was very quiet at the lighthouse that morning. Nothing but dirty plates and cups, and Chinese lanterns blowing in the breeze.

"Just like Matt to leave a mess," Rose mumbled.

"I can't hear Seagull," said Felix. And if Seagull was gone, where was Matt?

"Matt!" shouted Rose. "Maa-att!"

They went into the lighthouse and climbed the eighty-three steps up to the top.

"Matt, where are you hiding?" Rose panted.

But his room was empty. And the engine room with the great lamp was empty, too.

"He's gone," said Felix.

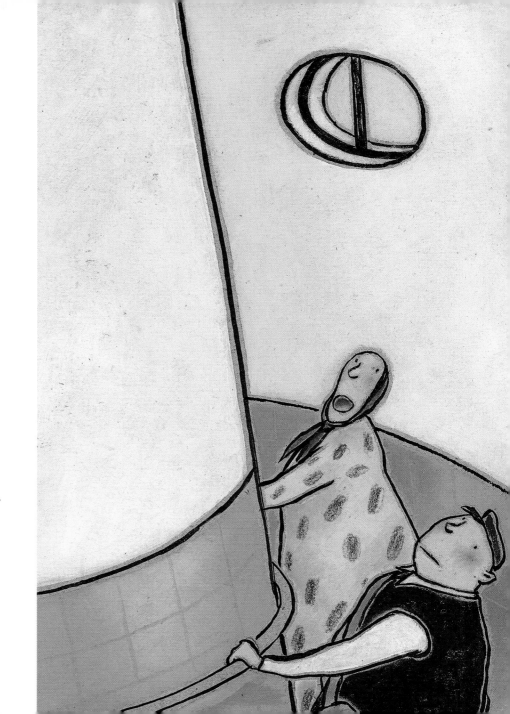

Rose still went to the lighthouse every day, just like before. Felix went, too, even though there were never any letters for Matt. Instead they leant on the railing and stared out to sea.

"He's gone off in a boat to look for Sailor," said Felix. "I bet that's it."

"He'll forget about us," said Rose, "when he's lying on a beach."

"Maybe he's been swallowed by a whale."

"Or his boat's been sunk."

"Or pirates have captured him."

Rose and Felix looked out at the ships on the sea.

Waiting for Matt to come home.